First American Edition 1998 Kane/Miller Book Publishers
Brooklyn, New York & La Jolla, California

Originally published in France under the title *Les Vacances de Roberta*
in 1996 by Editions du Seuil, Paris, France

Library of Congress Cataloging-in-Publication Data

Francia, Silvia.
(Vacances de Roberta. English)
Roberta's vacation / Silvia Francia. — 1st American ed.
p. cm.
Summary: While visiting her grandparents, Roberta the dog is bored so she sets off
alone for the beach, only to encounter a dog that scares her into hiding.
(1. Dogs—Fiction. 2. Beaches—Fiction. 3. Friendship—Fiction.) I. Title
PZ7.F84645Ro   1998   (E)—dc21   98-6604
ISBN 0-916291-83-9

Printed and bound in Singapore by Tien Wah Press Ltd.
1 2 3 4 5 6 7 8 9 10

Roberta's Vacation

Silvia Francia

Translated by Laura McKenna

A CRANKY NELL BOOK

Kane/Miller Book Publishers

Brooklyn, New York & La Jolla, California

Roberta is on vacation at Nanna and Gramps'.

Roberta is feeling quite bored today.
It's too hot to play, and besides, there's
no one to play with.

She'd like to go to the beach,
but her grandparents are taking a nap
and won't let her go alone.

"Too bad!" she says to herself. "I can't take this anymore. I'm going anyway!"

She takes some fizzy water with her,
because it's so hot outside.

The grand adventure begins!

Roberta walks and walks for a long, long time. Finally she's so pooped, she can't go any further.

"Hang in there, Roberta!" she tells herself.
"Just one more block, and you'll be at the
beach." But suddenly . . .

Whoooooooooooaaa! A horrible monster!

It's Jerome.

Roberta makes a mad dash
to the ocean.

"Whew! I lost him!"

She drinks some water to help her calm down.

"And why not take a little dip?" she thinks.
"Ahhhh! This is great! So refreshing!"

Then Roberta stretches out in a nice shady spot to take a nap.

"Uh-oh! Here comes Jerome. No need for him to see me!"

Schloop! She backs up into the drainpipe to hide.

In the meantime, Jerome makes himself comfortable . . .

. . . gobbling up his afternoon snack of
garlic sausages with lots of mustard.
When he's done, there's not a crumb left.

Before he's even had enough time to digest his food, splash! . . . he dives into the water.

Roberta, still hiding in the drainpipe, watches Jerome tossing about when suddenly . . .

. . . he disappears.

Gathering her courage,

Roberta jumps in to the rescue!

"What a lump!" says Roberta to herself. She's having a lot of trouble pulling him out of the water.

"You saved my life!" says Jerome, gasping for air. "Would you be my friend?"

And that was the beginning of a beautiful friendship.